Nettie Jo's Friends

BY PATRICIA C. McKISSACK
ILLUSTRATED BY SCOTT COOK

ALFRED A. KNOPF, NEW YORK

THIS IS A BORZOI BOOK
PUBLISHED BY ALFRED A. KNOPF, INC.

Designed by Mina Greenstein   Manufactured in Singapore

2   4   6   8   10   9   7   5   3

Library of Congress Cataloging-in-Publication Data
McKissack, Pat. Nettie Jo's friends.
Summary: Nettie Jo desperately needs a needle to sew
a new dress for her beloved doll, but the three animals
she helps during her search do not seem inclined to
give her their assistance in return.
[1. Animals—Fiction.   2. Dolls—Fiction]   I. Cook,
Scott, ill.   II. Title.
PZ7.M478693Ne   1989   [E]   87-14080
ISBN 0-394-89158-9
ISBN 0-394-99158-3 (lib. bdg.)

To Fred, Jr.
— P. C. M.

For Mama
— S. C.

And a special thanks to
Janet Schulman, Denise Cronin,
Mina Greenstein, and Anne Schwartz
— P. C. M.
S. C.

NETTIE JO was beside herself with excitement. Tomorrow was Cousin Willadeen and Charles Henry's wedding, and Nettie Jo was their flower girl.

"Hold still while I size this dress," Mama say, biting off a measure of thread.

Nettie Jo told herself to be still, but her legs kept bouncing up and down. "Annie Mae, we goin' to a wedding," she told her favorite doll.

"You can't take that ol' scraggly-looking doll," Mama put in. "Why, she's a mess, all tattered and such."

Nettie Jo's face dropped. "But Annie Mae is my friend. If she can't go, then I don't want to go either."

Mama smiled and winked her eye, saying, "I s'pose Annie Mae can come along and sit 'side of me, *if* she's wearing a new dress." Then she handed her daughter a piece of leftover lace material.

Nettie Jo's eyes brightened. "Thanks, Mama. Do you have an extra sewing needle?"

"Sorry. This'n is the only one I got, and I've got to finish your dress and mine by tonight. Try Granny."

Nettie Jo hurried to her grandmother's house. But Granny and all the aunts and cousins were busy putting the finishing touches on the wedding clothes. There wasn't an extra sewing needle anywhere in Briarsville.

Where can I get a needle? thought Nettie Jo.

In her favorite place by the sycamore tree, she came up with an idea.
Every winter high winds scattered things over McKelvey Bottoms, and
come spring Nettie Jo always went gathering the best stuff for her play
spot. "Girl," she say real confident-like, "I'm gon' go gathering and find

us a needle." And she tucked Annie Mae under her arm, slung her burlap
sack over her shoulder, and set out on her way.

She searched the rest of the morning and found a pretty red feather
along the road, a piece of ribbon in a hedge, and an old penny at the bus
depot. But no sewing needle.

"What we need is help," Nettie Jo decided, stopping in front of the bushes where Miz Rabbit lived.

Nettie Jo spoke politely. "Hello, Miz Rabbit. My cousin Willadeen and Charles Henry are getting married tomorrow. Annie Mae can't go to the wedding unless she has a new dress. But I need a sewing needle to stitch it up. Would you help us look for one?"

"What?" Miz Rabbit asked. "A wedding? A dress?" She was a mess of nerves, talking fast and hopping from foot to foot.

"Can't you hear?" Nettie Jo asked loudly.

Miz Rabbit shook her head wildly, then went on to explain how during the night her ears had flopped. "I must look terrible, dear me. And how will I hear when that dreadful Fox is coming?" Miz Rabbit never stopped talking.

Meanwhile, Nettie Jo studied on the things she had inside her sack.
"This ought to help you hear better," she say, pulling Miz Rabbit's
ears up and tying them with a piece of ribbon. Feeling satisfied,
Nettie Jo asked, "Can you hear now?"

"I—I believe, yes! And I think I hear that awful Fox coming." Miz Rabbit leaped away, chattering on and on about her woes.

"Wait! Wait! Fox is not coming," called Nettie Jo. "I need you to help me!" But it was too late. Miz Rabbit had scampered away.

"That's all right," Nettie Jo say, consoling Annie Mae. "We can find a needle by ourselves."

Searching in the big field, Nettie Jo found an empty spool and a hat. Down by the creek she found a brass button, a comb, and a thimble, but still no sewing needle. Then, in a hollow log near the mud bank, she come upon Fox's den. She could hear him stirrin' round inside. "Fox? I need your help something awful."

After explaining about the wedding and Annie Mae's dress and all, Nettie Jo asked, "Won't you help us look for a needle?"

Fox stumbled out of his den. *"Look?"* he grunted. "Humph! Look!" He tripped and bumped into things. "That's just it! I can't see nothing. Man, I been sleepin' in this dark den. Now the bright sunlight is blindin' me. My problem is how to see when Panther is lurkin' round."

Fox paced back and forward. Once again Nettie Jo studied on the
problem. From inside her sack she pulled out the hat and handed it to her
friend. "This will shade your eyes and help you see clearer."

Fox knocked a hard crease in the top, then broke down the brim over his left eye. He eased down to the creek and looked at himself in the dark water. "Just my style—sho-wa-do-wa-do-wa." Suddenly Fox stood still as a stone. "Look out! I think I spy Panther!" Then he dashed away.

Nettie Jo chased Fox all the way to the bridge. "No! Panther's not comin'!" she shouted. "Come back, Fox. Please, I need your help." But Fox didn't answer. He was long gone.

"Don't cry, Annie Mae." Nettie Jo hugged her doll up close. "We'll find a sewing needle...somewhere."

Nettie Jo stood on the bridge, wondering what to do next. The sun had moved around on the other side of the ridge. Not much daylight left. She'd searched along the road, past the bus depot, in the field, and by the creek. No needle. There wasn't but one other place to look—the woods. And Nettie Jo had never been inside the woods alone.

She thought about her problem, saying, "If I don't find a needle, Annie Mae, you can't go to the wedding. And if you can't go, I'm not going either!" Then, taking a deep breath, she walked into the woods.

It was cool and quiet among the trees. Nettie Jo was careful to stay on
the path, looking sharp for a sewing needle. But all she found was a lace
glove, a piece of rope, and a rusty horn. Then a bush rustled slightly, and
without another sound Panther appeared, moving like a big shadow.

Nettie Jo wanted to run but thought better of it. She held her head high and spoke right up. "How-do, Panther. You know, I really, really could use your help," she began like they were old friends, "you having such good eyesight an' all."

Panther mumbled something, but Nettie Jo rushed on, telling the big cat about the wedding and Annie Mae's dress and her long search for a sewing needle. "Will you help me look for one?" she asked.

Panther's yellow eyes narrowed to slits. Without making one sound, he sprang forward, opened his mouth, and—

"Ah-choo!" Panther sneezed.

"Oh, you've got a cold."

"Ah-ah-ah-ah-choo! How clever of you to notice," Panther growled hoarsely. "Worse still, I've lost my roar. And nobody's a-scared of a panther that can't roar." He flopped next to Nettie Jo, real disgusted-like.

"I'm so sorry," Nettie Jo say, looking inside her sack. Maybe she could help.

"Try this." She gave Panther the horn. He blew it.
Blat-a-tat-tum!
"It's not my roar, but it will do until I get my roar back."
"Now will you help me look for a sewing needle?"

"No time. No time," said Panther. "I've got to go chase Fox." And the
big cat bounded away, tooting his horn.

Blat-a-tat-tum! Blat-a-tat-tum!

"Oh, wait! Don't leave—I need your help."

But it was too late. Panther had vanished, and so had Nettie Jo's hopes of ever finding a sewing needle. It seemed almost for sure that Annie Mae wasn't going to the wedding, and that meant neither was Nettie Jo.

"You can cry now," Nettie Jo told her doll on the way home, " 'cause I am!"

Mama was still busy trying to finish all the sewing she had to do.
Nettie Jo sat by the cabin window, telling herself the wedding and the
pretty lace dress didn't matter.

Suddenly there was a big racket outside.

Blat-a-tat-tum! Blat-a-tat-tum!

Nettie Jo hurried to the door. Miz Rabbit rushed past. Hot on her
heels was Fox, and Panther was chasing them both.

Blat-a-tat-tum! Blat-a-tat-tum!

In the distance Nettie Jo heard their voices echoing through the bottom lands.

"We forgot something, little friend."

"*Thank you* for helping me hear better," said Miz Rabbit.

"*Thank you* for helping me see clearer," said Fox.

"*Thank you* for helping me roar louder," said Panther. "Might you be needing this?"

And a moonbeam caught a shiny thing as it fell to the ground. Nettie Jo hurried out to pick it up. It was a sewing needle! She smiled and spoke into the moon-washed night. "Thank you, my friends."

Then, hugging Annie Mae, she skipped back inside the cabin, humming "Here comes the bride."